D1607784

BEYOND THE ECLIPSE

STORIES OF LIFE, LOSS, AND HOPE

ALICE THORPE HARROLD

InspïringVoices®
A Service of **Guideposts**

Scripture taken from the New King James Version. Copyright 1979, 1980, 1982 by Thomas Nelson, inc. Used by permission. All rights reserved.

Cover by FOSTER BARKER CREATIVE INC

Photography by Garry E. Hodges

Inspiring Voices books may be ordered through booksellers or by contacting:

Inspiring Voices
1663 Liberty Drive
Bloomington, IN 47403
www.inspiringvoices.com
1 (866) 697-5313

Because of the dynamic nature of the Internet, any web addresses or links contained in this book may have changed since publication and may no longer be valid. The views expressed in this work are solely those of the author and do not necessarily reflect the views of the publisher, and the publisher hereby disclaims any responsibility for them.

Any people depicted in stock imagery provided by Thinkstock are models, and such images are being used for illustrative purposes only.
Certain stock imagery © Thinkstock.

ISBN: 978-1-4624-0870-2 (sc)
ISBN: 978-1-4624-0872-6 (hc)
ISBN: 978-1-4624-0871-9 (e)

Library of Congress Control Number: 2013923533

Printed in the United States of America.

Inspiring Voices rev. date: 1/20/2014

Written from the heart to those for whom the
word good-bye comes much too soon…

CONTENTS

INTRODUCTION

My inspiration to create words upon lines of paper oftentimes occurs in the dark of night, perhaps the optimum time to hear what God places upon my heart.

My journey began when we lost our nineteen-year-old son, Adam, to cancer. Creating this book became God's gift when a future so secure had vanished and the road leading toward tomorrow was no longer bathed in light. I discovered within my spirit that unspoken words still held messages of hope and encouragement. Adam's photograph on a perfect summer's day became the catalyst for the first story, "The Young Fisherman."

It was my prayer as I penned the words tenderly held upon these pages that solace, wisdom, strength, and even forgiveness would belong to the reader, that the God of the universe would reveal those luminous strands of joy that exist beyond sorrow and loss.

As days become years, the beloved sun has once again slipped into view, revealing its brilliance as impenetrable darkness moves silently away. *Beyond the Eclipse* becomes the perfect illustration of the times when life comes full circle.

CHAPTER 1

BEYOND THE ECLIPSE . . . WHERE COMFORT IS RECEIVED

Blessed are those who mourn, For they shall be comforted.
—Matthew 5:4

The Young Fisherman

The photograph lovingly held in a frame of silver stands silently on the bedside table. It captures for all eternity the young man and his fish. The sky seems to reach down and caress the wind-tossed hair as the clouds but for a moment are still. The familiar khaki shorts, the bare feet, the boats moored in the background—all part of an endless summer day.

Perhaps the picture is so cherished because that day did end. The sunshine that was captured on film became elusive as the young man faced his foe of cancer. It was a battle hard fought, but the victory was not to be his. As I ponder the photograph of a son forever nineteen, I begin to see far beyond that summer's day.

In the treasured whisper, "Follow Me, and I will make you fishers of men" (Matthew 4:19), I am blessed to watch the promise unfold. You see, the quiet faith that gently held our young fisherman struck a chord deep within those whose lives he touched. They watched the road he was called to travel and saw strength only his God could give. On the darkest of days they became transformed by memories of a life worth living.

Because of his journey and unwavering faith, Adam truly became a fisher of men long after this photograph was taken. Friends who surrounded him in those last days blessed each of us with their comforting presence as they in turn found solace. His beloved sister wrote these words from a heart forever changed: "Adam was my hero, my mentor... everything I wanted to be. I have now placed my life in God's hands."

One by one his God *has* become theirs as the sun's rays dance upon the photograph with its frame of silver.

Father, I cherish the words placed within my heart about our son, Adam, and his beloved photograph. Thank You for the encouragement to create *Beyond the Eclipse* after his journey found its final destination at Your side. I give praise for the revelation that a life well lived has immeasurable value, no matter how brief. Please hold those who mourn, those surrounded by darkness, and those who find themselves on a road not chosen safely within the hollow of Your hand. Amen and amen.

Adam Always Liked You Best

His world was limited in its dimensions until you became part of the fabric. Even though we were there, responding to his first smile, the beginning reaches of those tiny hands, and every tentative new step, there was still something missing. From the first picture drawn, he instinctively knew this tiny baby was one of God's greatest treasures meant just for him! Earlier days filled with predictable endings and beginnings now felt transformed with new interweavings of laughter and sunshine. Your smile touched the heart of your brother and inspired his walk toward the future. At long last he had someone to guide on this journey called life, someone to protect when the world came too close, and someone to see him as perfect!

Adam always liked you best

His love of the beach intensified when he shared it with you—the shells, the birds, the sand castles, a boat simply called the Mako.

Lifelong friendships took a distant second to the kinship so gently nurtured within your hearts. Memories of go-carts, a family adventure to faraway Russia, and the curve of the staircase on Christmas morning— all part of time continuing its journey toward tomorrow.

Adam always liked you best

Even as the road took him to a faraway city in search of medical answers, the darkness was kept at bay by your presence, your touch, and your prayers. It was a sister's love that reassured him when the sun lost its brilliance.

He truly understood that the child he cherished from the very beginning would one day fulfill all he saw within her spirit.

There was never any doubt, Adam always liked you best!

Lord, the beloved scribble in Adam's coloring book became the foundation of this story. A baby girl cradled in a seat was the perfect picture to carefully bring home from kindergarten for his newborn sister, Adrian. That scribble now graces the room of her child. Always bring to our remembrances those blessings and gifts You have bestowed upon us. Forgive us the times we forget to cherish treasures that have been so lovingly given. Amen.

A Vase of Bronze

Embraced by the winter cold, a cemetery vase gently holds a single pine bough. The starkness seems out of place among the blanket of Christmas poinsettias and lush evergreens, yet its simplicity has the ability to draw those passing by. One wonders what significance this pine bough possesses to stand so tall within the vessel of bronze.

Christmas Day whispers facets of the story like a shared secret. This bough comes from a stately tree that touches the past. The one who tenderly placed it within the bronze vase is an elderly gentleman bending in stature. Gnarled hands that have embraced a lifetime cradled the branch as though it were a treasure of immeasurable wealth.

Memories stir, giving an aching heart pause as he recalls the pine as a seedling. It seems but a brief journey in time when a young couple planted it in the soil, awaiting the future where dreams danced and hope beckoned.

Years have passed with a blend of joy and sorrow, laughter and tears. Grown children have lives of their own, and friends are a precious few. He walks slowly now on paths where deer find safe haven and a red fox awaits the dusk.

Deep within the forest is the tree of his youth, one all but touching the sky with its majestic presence. The beloved tree is able to reach beyond its own boundaries to bestow a gift upon those who tenderly cared for it. From its span, the bough was taken, proudly gracing the grave of one who helped nurture it—one who has for a moment slipped away from those who love her still.

Father, my walks through Adam's cemetery bring remembrances of those who have been at my side. You used the simplicity of that bronze vase for the crux of this story. I knew the solitary pine bough had to have been of significance for one to place it within the urn. Gifts, such as this bough, sometimes appear in the most unlikely places! Thank You for comfort as we move through the days still before us. Amen.

Susan's Gift

The treasures that beckon beneath the Christmas tree hold one's imagination captive. Do ribbons conceal a gift that fulfills a wish or reach into the very soul of one blessed to receive it? A treasure has many facets. It can grace a hearth where fires dance or take one on a journey through the depths of imagination.

One special gift tucked so neatly under glittering lights reflects something carefully chosen. This antique wooden box encased in tissue paper will be perfect wherever it is placed.

However, knowing my beloved friend as I do, I have learned her desires have become the desires of God's heart. She genuinely cherishes that which cannot be held within a worldly treasure, no matter how beautiful. She is blessed with the revelation that all which is sought is not nestled among well-appointed packages and holiday laughter.

As time moves toward a future unknown but secure, this well-worn treasure will hold mementos of hopes and dreams. When days find her remembering those who have walked at her side, I pray she will gently tuck reminders of those memories inside this gift. It has ample room for jewels of the heart.

When the future becomes the present, she can take comfort in knowing that the one who bestowed this gift upon her will always care, always cherish her, and will forever praise the King in the manger for such a beloved friend. Christmas joy!

Father, You gave Jesus the cherished gift of friends, among them John, Peter, Lazarus, and Matthew. You also bless us with those who walk at our side. We are grateful for the sincerity, solace, and wisdom they bring to each day. Make us mindful of the many situations they face. We boldly ask that You place within our hearts godly words to comfort and encourage them. Amen.

The Unsaid Good-Bye

In the solemn halls outside the beautifully appointed office, the silence seems to speak volumes. The empty chair within stands as though it is awaiting the one who has always graced it. Cheryl, our beloved church secretary, made her heavenward journey home... quietly, quickly.

It seems she left without looking back. Did she speak? Did we fail to hear the word *good-bye*... or was it so softly spoken we missed it?

Perhaps, as believers, words of farewell do not hold credence. If we truly walk upon the road we profess, being but sojourners in a foreign land, then *good-bye* is not part of our world. We still have a homecoming on the horizon.

We simply walk on this side of time and yearn to cross a span that cannot be measured. One day in the blink of an eye, we will stand at the throne of the One who has never ceased to love a world that is but temporal.

We never heard her say good-bye. With assurance, we will continue to await a tomorrow that holds no end, a tomorrow that encompasses the cloud of believers who have journeyed ahead.

Lord, You know the sorrow hearts carry as we continue this journey through life. How we miss our friend! Her unexpected death serves as a valuable lesson that tomorrow is not assured, not given. Enable us to hold tightly to the promise of eternity where the spoken word good-bye will cease to exist. Amen.

Treasures of the Heart

Memories are like glimpses through the flames of a hearth's fire. Some are so vivid in clarity that they take one's breath away; others seem almost opaque like smoke. These recollections appear so briefly one must wonder if they happened or were part of the imagination.

Sometimes in the stillness of the night, embers of the fire have a richness that ignites the soul. The heart delights in its treasures, and memories surface like flames. The vividness of colors draws one back to a time that seems so long ago yet imminent like yesterday.

Memories are gifts of the Father to His beloved children, easing the burden of loss that threatens to overwhelm. They are the compelling desire to relive and recapture those times now threatening to smolder and fade.

It seems like yesterday when carnations graced a vase on Valentine's Day, bringing beauty into a room where questions went unanswered and prayers seemed unheard. While a family struggled with an illness that for a season eclipsed all else, God made His presence known through the love of those who watched and cared.

Nurses, almost his contemporaries, went above and beyond their duties to acquire and then sign a valentine card from the young man to his parents. They instinctively knew that had his illness not occurred, he would have sent the perfect, quirky card. That last valentine card so tenderly forged, "Love, Adam," becomes the treasure that warms a heart threatening to grow cold. Other memories, like tears, flow and heal. The stuffed monkey, a whimsical gift adorned with a satin heart, represents a life of normalcy, laughter, and love. His girlfriend, Katie, brought this larger-than-life creature into his room along with a smile that dispelled the sadness. Her presence by his side reassured everyone that this road was not walked alone. These treasures are now forgotten except by those who were players in a scene from a life now out of reach.

It truly is a balance. Life dictates we live in the present, bringing shattered dreams into the light of reality, yet the heart finds safe haven in the burning embers of the past.

The past—two thousand years ago—and Mary comes to mind, where common threads of motherhood and loss are shared. Did she also allow memories to intrude upon her thoughts, to ease the tears? One must wonder if she often recalled the night when angels sang and shepherds sought.

Did she reminisce about the time her beloved Son remained in the temple, while she journeyed home, the anguish of separation blending with the relief of laughter as she was reunited with her child? Did memories when He walked by her side carry her through empty days?

Memories do recall moments now past. They can encourage, but must be lovingly held in the heart as treasures, not substituted for life itself. One must be very cautious, as the past is not inhabitable.

Remember, we were created to bring glory to God, to trust Him even when the present echoes with emptiness and the future looms dark. If Mary had chosen the past, remaining in her haven of memories, she would have missed the resurrection. She would have missed the victory of life over death. Instead, looking up and then ahead, Mary became the quintessential role model.

Those who have journeyed through the past hold the ability to forever change us. We behold truth as the embers of faith are fanned into flames, illuminating the way for believers.

Father, we are grateful for fond memories. They warm the heart and forbid the cold from finding a permanent home. They serve as reminders of precious gifts with which Your children have been blessed. Amen.

CHAPTER 2

BEYOND THE ECLIPSE . . . WHERE FORGIVENESS IS FOUND

Blessed is he whose transgression is forgiven, Whose sin is covered.
—Psalm 32:1

A Creation Made New

As one glimpses winter in its slumber, the promise of God's new creation seems elusive. The beautiful textures of spring that dance and blend into summer are silent. Trees reach toward heaven with branches bare. Bushes that once swayed in a symphony of color stand mute. The colorless days challenge the words *new creation.* The gray of the earth seems to echo in lives around us. One does not have to look far to see a heart yearning for what is out of reach—a mind overflowing with memories to ease empty hours and endless days.

Come, journey with me back to the time of Jesus. It was an age that also held hopelessness, when grayness touched lives and tears flowed. Scripture has the unique ability to weave words so that the past can be seen as a reflection of today. Sit back and let the din of the crowds and dust of the roads draw you. Walk with those who lived long ago.

Our first encounter is the woman at the well. Remember her? She is despised and scorned! Her journey in the heat of the day is one of necessity to avoid the cruel taunts of those who deem her unworthy. You see, her lifestyle brings judgment, as she married five times and now lives with a man not her husband.

Contemplate the reflection of her life in our world today. Some see themselves as that woman—alone, judged, burdened by a sadness that seems to penetrate one's very soul. Survival is assured by donning a cloak of hardness to protect a heart all but broken.

Others stand at the well and assume the role of judge as *their* climb upon a pedestal begins. Each word uttered is a step:

Sinner

Fallen

Lowly

Adulteress

Take heed, beloved. It is *that same pedestal* that keeps those who would judge from standing beside the Savior. You see, He came to reach out, to comfort, to forgive. Sometimes in the still of a moment, even on a winter's day, one is transformed. As she stands by His side, her heart changes, and she becomes a new creation. This woman, who ventured out only when solitude was assured, becomes the catalyst to draw others to Christ. Her bold words, "Come, see a Man who told me all things that I ever did. Could this be the Christ?" (John 4:29), truly bring life to those who would listen. They are given the choice to climb down from their pedestals and respond. His whisper across eternity can be heard, "Behold, I make all things new" (Revelation 21:5).

Our journey along dusty roads continues toward an encounter with the prodigal son. For some, he is the child that lives in the heart. Choices made have taken him far from those who will always love him. The laughter that once rang out is silenced by distance.

In our era, some might sympathize with his brother. After all, he is the dutiful son, the one who stayed. The joy his father feels at the return of his brother eludes him. He will remain in winter as long as jealousy and bitterness harden his heart.

For others, the reflection of the prodigal becomes reality. They see themselves as those who walked away in search of all life had to offer. Returning empty-handed and without hope, their father, their heavenly Father, welcomes them with open arms. Truly in His presence they, too, are *new creations*, leaving the old in lives now past.

The reflections mirrored in the Holy Scripture are different in each life. Whether one stands by the well or far above on a pedestal, whether one experiences firsthand the walk of the prodigal or relates to the heart of his brother, one can draw ever so near as to hear the Master's footsteps.

Our journey comes to a close. The dust that once coated the Carpenter's sandals becomes part of memory along with lives forever changed. Forgiveness is found through the parting words, "Therefore, if anyone is in Christ, he is a new creation; old things have passed away; behold, all things have become new" (2 Corinthians 5:17). We are blessed by the fulfillment of this promise!

Father, the gentle touch of Your hand reassures us the old truly has passed away. As surely as spring follows winter, we know this journey ends at Your side. Amen.

A Remnant of Cloth

There exists a remnant of cloth that weaves from the swaddling clothes of the newborn Messiah toward the fulfillment of prophecy. One can truly visualize it becoming the robe on the One who touched and healed before its ultimate transformation as the burial garb of the Savior in His tomb.

Is it just fabric, or is it what binds lives together? Is it material that turns to dust with the passage of time, or is it the raiment of righteousness?

Its appeal captivates. It is all one would hope for, need, or desire. The price—the sacrifice of a man, God's own Son. Too much! Too much! How could one ever be worthy of such a cost?

As the memory of the remnant with its beginnings in the manger wraps around our lives, we find worthiness and forgiveness. That same fabric that bound the Father to His beloved Son holds us forever secure.

Father, even as these words resound, "The price… God's own Son… too much, too much!," the debt has been satisfied, reminding us of an unending love. Thank You for a generosity that transcends our human imagination. Amen.

David's Psalm

Psalm 32 is David's Psalm. How it echoes the relationship that existed between the shepherd boy and the God of the universe! One can imagine laughter filling those days, moving like a breeze across the still lake, causing the surface to dance.

To some, this early relationship between the young boy and his God mirrors their own walk with the Master. God's presence is so assured that they have only to reach out to know they are loved. The throne is there, and the road is clear and straight. To others, however, the throne appears distant. The road, clouded with shadows and darkness, is far less visible—the same road yet two diverse viewpoints. For some it's inviting. For others it is almost impassable.

Is it the perspective of the sojourner? Are we all at different points in our Christian walk? Is it accessible to all who believe? God gently reminds us that His beloved shepherd boy, the one who was dear to His own heart, also knew darkness. His human choices placed him on a road no longer bathed in light. David became a lost sheep during his entangled relationship with Bathsheba, as the darkness of sin and murder encumbered the way to his heavenly Father.

Take heart! These words of the psalmist act as a balm for the aching soul. I acknowledged my sin to You, And my iniquity I have not hidden. I said, "I will confess my transgressions to the Lord," And You forgave the iniquity of my sin (Psalm 32:5).

Do you see it? Acknowledgment of sin allows us to bring it out of the darkness and into the light.

By seeking forgiveness from the One who knows us intimately, we can walk out of the shadows. If we are very quiet, we can hear the precious whisper of Jesus, "I am the light of the world. He who follows Me shall not walk in darkness, but have the light of life" (John 8:12).

We can experience the truth David wove throughout his psalm. "Blessed is he whose transgression is forgiven, Whose sin is covered" (Psalm 32:1).

God, we are grateful for truth and faithfulness. Gently remind us when darkness threatens and we feel like lost sheep that You, who neither slumbers nor sleeps, hold us securely in the hollow of Your powerful hand. Amen.

The Prodigal

The Bible lesson was "The Prodigal." My obligation was to present it in a manner that would bring meaning to each of the generations represented within our church circle.

The focus centered on rebellion and a young woman who had rejected her parents and their values. Identifying with a willful and disobedient child was difficult, as we had been blessed with children who brought joy into each day. Our daughter, so different from the portrayal of this young woman, cares deeply for others. Her ability to reach out and comfort those tossed by life's demands and sorrows has made a difference in an unyielding world.

Perhaps by weaving this study around the prodigal son and his rejection of his father, I could better connect with the moral dilemma. Not to be! I had been blessed with a son whose focus was on others and remained thus throughout his life.

Finally I took my pursuit to the Father. Our unique relationship as believers allows us to kneel at His feet and seek answers. His wisdom illuminated a truth that had eluded me. I walked among the prodigals. I was one of them! A lesson to be taught became one learned as the word *prodigal* wrapped around me like a shroud.

I had set aside the scripture from Deuteronomy 6:4–7:

> Hear, O Israel: The Lord our God, the Lord is one! You shall love the Lord your God with all your heart, with all your soul, and with all your strength. And these words, which I command you today, shall be in your heart. You shall teach them diligently to your children,

and shall talk of them when you sit in your house, when you walk by the way, when you lie down, and when you rise up.

I had failed to take our children to church, to share with them about God. I was the one who had walked away.

When I found my way back, overwhelmed by sorrow, my heavenly Father welcomed me with arms that forever have the ability to hold and to heal.

When the world batters believers with words and pronouncements that say there is no hope, the darkness can be kept at bay by a relationship that transcends all others. Our heavenly Father is waiting, His mercy and grace limitless. He truly does rejoice over each lost sheep that is found.

Father, You loved this world enough to sacrifice Your own Son. For each prodigal and those who love them, that is a gift of immeasurable wealth! Amen.

The Voice Within

The voice within is sometimes but a whisper slipping through one's thoughts without a trace. At other times its volume overshadows each thought and every prayer!

We know we are forgiven, yet the voice within whispers reminders of a past road upon which we stumbled and fell.

We say we belong to Him, yet that same small voice reveals images of anger, frustration, and impatience.

We profess forgiveness toward another and then find it is one thing to forgive and quite another to forget. The voice stirs up emotions that make us question our ability to walk at His side.

Beloved, when that inward voice, that human voice challenges all you know to be true, listen to God in the silence. With His words upon your heart, confidence and hope will become cherished companions on this journey called life.

Father, when our inner voice threatens to overshadow the truth we glean from Holy words, we ask for wisdom and faith, knowing You are forever at our side. Amen.

Thirty Pieces of Silver

The going rate of betrayal was thirty pieces of silver. How does one place a price on turning away when another's needs are so great? Where is the value when denials are spoken and a solitary figure faces Calvary alone, forsaken?

As millenniums pass, whispers of "Thou shalt not" from the Ten Commandments continue to be at odds with the will of men. Each word becomes a coin within this pouch of leather, weighing down the very souls of those who profess to walk at His side. There are coins that represent adultery, covetousness, and unbelief—coins that portray blasphemy, selfishness, and an unwillingness to forgive.

You see, betrayal is not always the willful turning away from someone. It can also exist in more subtle ways. Man's nature enables coins to resound against each other within the leather pouch. Its very weight mirrors the clash between man's desires to do what is right and his human frailty. This burden of silver exacts a toll from those who claim Calvary would find them at His side. The path one desires to journey seems at times overshadowed by a darkening world that insists on its own way!

Take heart, beloved. In the glorious Easter sunrise, the hands that bear scars of nails driven reach into each life, each soul. With the word *forgiven*, possibilities are endless. One has only to surrender the infamous pouch by the foot of the cross. It can no longer be a burden if the coins have been replaced by joy and salvation.

Lord, with the words "Go forth, forgiven, and praise Your Creator for a debt paid in full," we place this pouch of leather at Your feet. We give praise that the burden no longer encumbers us on this journey called life. Amen.

CHAPTER 3

BEYOND THE ECLIPSE . . . WHERE WISDOM IS REVEALED

He gives wisdom to the wise and knowledge
to those who have understanding.
—Daniel 2:21

A Life of Promise

Tears fall from those yet unborn, as their fate is determined. Oh, Father, have we moved so far from You that we would halt a life before it begins? Do we know what we miss? With laughter stilled and a smile unfinished, talents lost and a hug never to be felt, we face the truth of a life never to be lived.

The questions resound: *A choice? Whose choice?*

Oh, Lord, the laughter would have brought joy to a hurting world. The smile would have warmed the heart. Those talents could have broadened horizons while hugs would have given solace and encouragement. The words now silenced would have given dreams flight, and a life could have been lived for God's own glory.

Voices whisper: *A choice? Whose choice?*

In the quiet of the night, the answer echoes, "Man's," and tears still fall.

Father, when choices made build walls that seem to conceal Your presence, when our mirrors reflect brokenness and regret, remind us that is why You sent the Savior. We are truly blessed to be seen as forgiven and holy through His gift of life. Amen.

Hannah's Prayer

As one reads through the Old Testament and the book of 1 Samuel, Hannah's conversation with her Lord can be heard, "O Lord of hosts, if You will indeed look on the affliction of Your maidservant, and remember me, and not forget Your maidservant, but will give Your maidservant a male child, then I will give him to the Lord all the days of his life, and no razor shall come upon his head"(1 Samuel 1:11).

Hannah's prayer cannot help but touch us as the tears hidden in her heart become a spring that wells up within her very soul. The vision of her kneeling before God crosses the centuries, becoming a reminder of our own prayer life.

Prayers truly are as varied as the lives of those who pray. Some are outpourings of anguish, need, and pain. Others are pleas to untangle knots we have tied, to ask forgiveness when temptations are greater than willpower, and to seek solace when words spoken in anger inflict hurt.

As we reflect upon prayers and the promises that accompany them, we would do well to focus not only on the gifts sought from our Creator—the gifts of healing, reconciliation, answers, and peace—but on the Giver. As His beloved children, we must trust that He truly knows what is best. When we sincerely pray, "Thy will be done," that is faith.

Father, we encounter days when questions have no answers, when hurt is crushing, and promises made fall short. Gently remind us that we are Yours, imperfect yet set apart, because You have called us to Yourself. Amen

The Golden Thread

Winter, an ever-changing tapestry with threads woven together as the endless gray days blend one into another. Dark ominous clouds seem forever in motion, serving as backdrops for tree branches that wait silently and unadorned.

At times, these grays and browns echo the human heart where hope seems elusive and joy out of reach. Prayers, rather than flowing effortlessly, seem empty and unheard. We sense a pattern of dark colors not unlike winter within our own lives.

Jesus knew our tapestries would hold threads of sorrow, emptiness, and doubt. He understood that desires of the heart would fail. With wisdom, He taught a precious lesson which would strengthen and uplift His children. With the beloved words, "Our Father" (Matthew 6:9-13), He began this prayer that would become a golden thread, intertwining and weaving throughout the darkness.

> Our Father in heaven,
> Hallowed be Your name.
> Your kingdom come.
> Your will be done
> On earth as it is in heaven.
> Give us this day our daily bread.
> And forgive us our debts,
> As we forgive our debtors.
> And do not lead us into temptation,
> But deliver us from the evil one.

For Yours is the kingdom and the power and the glory forever. Amen

When whispered from the heart, The Lord's Prayer enables you to look up in praise and walk forward in faith!

Father, Your Son gave us this cherished prayer. We ask Your Holy Spirit to breathe life into it as our hearts embrace these words with their threads of gold. Amen

The Kaleidoscope

As the brass cylinder turns and the colors blend one into another, the seeker barely pauses before turning the instrument to another view.

As one looks forward to the vibrant colors of fall on the horizon, perhaps missed is the beauty of today. Is the seeker forever seeking what is elusive while overlooking what is?

The Gospel echoes these words, "Therefore do not worry about tomorrow, for tomorrow will worry about its own things. Sufficient for the day is its own trouble" (Matthew 6:34). We would do well to reflect upon this day, this hour, and the Creator, who so lovingly bestowed it.

Ponder the whispered scripture, "This is the day the Lord has made; We will rejoice and be glad in it" (Psalm 118:24). Perhaps we could simply enjoy the mosaics as they appear in the kaleidoscope without wondering how all would look with yet another turn.

Maybe, just maybe we could take time to walk with our Creator through this day and this hour, leaving tomorrow in His unchanging, capable hands!

Father, gently touch hearts that yearn. Remind us that as life's kaleidoscope moves from view to view, You are the one true constant in our lives. Amen.

The Shepherd among His Flock

The hallowed walls of God's church invite those from every walk of life.

Within the sanctuary some are met with reverence. They have found favor and success by the world's standards. Any needs that arise are generously met through their wealth and compassion. The respect shown them is genuine and heartfelt.

Others arrive with few taking notice, as if these people are almost invisible. Their demeanors mirror the reality of jobs lost and money scarce. A few nod in their direction before they seek out familiar faces. It is intriguing to observe love, respect, and possibly subtle judgment walking hand in hand within this sacred assembly. Watch and listen.

"For where two or three are gathered together in My name, I am there in the midst of them!" The time-honored scripture from Matthew 18:20 reveals the presence of another in the sanctuary. One wonders if anyone senses His presence as people make their ways to favorite pews. The rustling of the Shepherd's robe and the sound of His sandals can certainly be imagined as He moves across these polished floors. His majesty enables Him to see beyond wealth, further than weariness and tattered clothing.

He approaches His own, knowing them as they truly are rather than how they appear. He sees those who walked with Him through the dark of night. They know His touch and have seen His faithfulness when life was without hope. He is well aware that their spirits claim the words from Jeremiah 32:38, "They shall be My people, and I will be their God." They bow their heads, acknowledging the One who loves them unconditionally.

He moves effortlessly among those who seek as they consider the promises in Matthew 7:7, "Ask, and it will be given to you; seek, and you will find; knock, and it will be opened to you." They sense His presence as they come to the realization there is emptiness that neither success nor financial gain can fill. The future yawns before them like a dark chasm, and they know in their hearts there has to be more. Deeply moved by the gentleness of the Lord's Prayer, they humbly beseech God to forgive their transgressions against those they have wronged. With the sacred truth echoed in Matthew, they find this very morning that which they have sought.

There are many within the sanctuary cherishing their relationships with the faithful Shepherd. However, the yearning in His eyes remains as He watches those who have relegated Him to an era now past. Pursuits of the right connections and financial power have taken precedence in lives seeking earthly treasures. They overlook the very One who spoke the universe into existence, yet He patiently remains within reach. His call upon lives has not ceased.

The parable of the lost sheep is the perfect sermon with its timely words:

> For the Son of Man has come to save that which was lost. What do you think? If a man has a hundred sheep, and one of them goes astray, does he not leave the ninety-nine and go to the mountains to seek the one that is straying? And if he should find it, assuredly, I say to you, he rejoices more over that sheep than over the ninety-nine that did not go astray. Even so it is not the will of your Father who is in heaven that one of these little ones should perish. (Matthew 18:11–14)

As the hour draws to a close, the church bells chime. The congregation crosses over the threshold and into the world that waits. Another Sunday, another opportunity for eternal life, and one more chance to walk with the Shepherd.

If you truly concentrate, you can watch Him longingly gaze after those who don't look back . . .

Father, You know us intimately as we share thoughts, prayers, and hopes. With boldness, we beseech You to open eyes that remain closed and soften hearts that seem so unyielding. Enable us to be still enough to behold the Shepherd in our midst and humble enough to embrace those we have yet to call friends. Amen.

Choices

We need to slow our pace as time moves forward and reflect upon simple words. Luke 2:25 tells of a man in Jerusalem whose name was Simeon, a man just and devout. What remarkable words to describe someone! In Luke 2:26–27, the verse continues with the revelation the Holy Spirit had imparted to Simeon, "And it had been revealed to him that he would not see death before he had seen the Lord's Christ."

The fulfillment of this message came to pass! The cradling of this beloved child, Jesus, was the culmination of faith, hope, and steadfastness for God's righteous servant. It is not hard to imagine the pounding of his heart as he held the baby gently in his arms. The jubilant prayer of thanksgiving within Luke 2:28–30 resounded throughout the temple, "Lord, now You are letting Your servant depart in peace, According to Your word; For my eyes have seen your salvation!" There was neither doubt nor hesitancy in Simeon's declaration. He recognized the Messiah; He knew the child he held close to his heart was the One promised.

A world that for so long had awaited the Messiah would now have to choose—recognize and accept Him… or reject Him. That decision still remains in the soft whisper in Matthew 16:15 when He said to His disciples, "But who do you say that I am?"

Some see only a baby in a manger. They see a carpenter who transforms wood, a good man unfairly placed upon the cross.

For others the choice is life-changing. They recognize the Messiah in that manger. They know this carpenter transforms lives. As they view Calvary, they remember the centurion's words, "Truly this Man was the Son of God" (Mark 15:39), and they understand the ultimate sacrifice. The thankfulness of hearts overflows into lives.

One encounter with the Messiah… two choices but an eternal answer!

Father, the words 'just and devout' have extraordinary depth. We know our lives could echo those words through Your Holy Spirit's guidance. Grant us godly wisdom when we are making choices and let our lives mirror those decisions. In Christ's name, amen.

CHAPTER 4

BEYOND THE ECLIPSE . . . WHERE TRUTH IS ILLUMINATED

Jesus said, "I am the way and the truth and the life. No
one comes to the Father except through Me."
—John 14:6

A Choice of Stone

The name *Jesus Christ* rolls off the tongue with hardly a thought, and those who love Him hear nails driven. The world boasts of its treasures while His own feel the crown of thorns pressing down. The words of God become simply that—*words* with no thought to the One who stands vigilantly behind them.

When did those He created wander so far that morality faded into the distance? What journey could possibly have been so compelling that compassion was forgotten? Perhaps the answer lies within hearts that refuse to believe in things unseen, hearts of stone.

For those who never cease to await His return, the truth of His existence is etched in stone as well—a tomb of stone… and a stone simply rolled away.

Lord, fill our hearts with prayer and compassion, not judgment, for those to whom Your name continues to be just that… a name. Touch them and change them while reminding Your children that You did no less for them. Amen.

A Garden Prayer

As we slip into the garden, we are drawn to the figure of the humble carpenter. His prayers for those who surround Him in His last hours reveal the tender intimacy He shares with His heavenly Father. His heart is interceding for those who will not walk these last miles but vanish into the darkness as if they had never known Him.

The words of the one praying never cease. You see, He knows His own. He is well aware of their human frailties. He knows there will be denials, that fear will overshadow faith, and that believers yet to come will face their own dark nights.

His next words come so softly one must strain to hear, "I pray from them. I do not pray for the world but for those whom You have given Me, for they are Yours" (John 17:9).

It is sometimes overwhelming to realize that God's words would be shared with us because those early disciples chose to witness. Because of Calvary, the world would be given a choice—to walk in belief or walk away.

The garden beckons.

Father, we are thankful for the faithfulness of those first disciples. We have believed through their words and count ourselves among Your children. Words cannot fully express our gratitude that Jesus would include us in His prayer. We are overwhelmed that His thoughts in those last hours would be of us. Amen.

A Man Possessed

He ran down dusty roads, alone and weary. The demons that drove him among the tombs were never still, never quiet, tormenting his every breath.

He experienced a darkness that truly engulfed him, shutting out a world where hope was said to live. The evil within was so strong it could snap chains and break fetters. That same evil could wrap so tightly around his thoughts that they were never free.

Beloved, when hope seems gone, remember the Holy Scripture whispers of a road no longer dark, no longer lonely.

It was upon this road that a tormented man met his gentle savior. With the words, "Come out of the man, unclean spirit" (Mark 5:8), a transformation took place, as the darkness in his soul was banished. The man who once stood alone now possessed the most cherished of all relationships. You see, one cannot encounter the Savior and not be changed!

Lord, each life You touch is a life reborn. It is our prayer that this world will continue to be transformed by the Savior's gentle hand. Amen.

Reflections

A new year has dawned!

I wonder, as the old year was placed among our memories much like ornaments tucked away for another season, did anyone praise God for His faithfulness? As Times Square sparkled with revelry and the ball made its journey downward, did anyone think to look up?

As people shared and celebrated, did anyone sense His presence? When fireworks danced on the horizon, lighting up the night, did anyone reflect upon the Light of the World?

We must be aware that just as ice coats the branches of an evergreen, weighing them down, a day without the fellowship of our Creator leaves the soul cold and apart. All the lights, celebrations, and festivities cannot fill that void.

He waits in the quiet when noise abounds. He patiently tends His sheep and longs for those who have wandered. His words remind us that in a world that lives for today, He is there for eternity.

We give praise, Father, for the miracle of this new year! Enable us to walk in the light of Your love and seek Your presence. We humbly ask that holy words will warm hearts and enrich lives. Grant us the revelation to make a difference in each of these 365 days. Amen.

Shepherds and Lambs

Christmas brings reflections of angels, shepherds, and the child in the manger. Time and again we have heard the story of the shepherds tending their flocks. God's word illuminates the angel's proclamation found in Luke 2:10–12, "Do not be afraid, for behold, I bring you good tidings of great joy which will be to all people. For there is born to you this day in the city of David a savior, who is Christ the Lord. And this will be the sign to you: You will find a Babe wrapped in swaddling cloths, lying in a manger." We are blessed to share the truth of that night so long ago in which lives were forever changed.

How precious that the angels would appear to shepherds. How fitting those shepherds would go in search of the babe, the *Lamb* of God!

Heavenly Father, make us mindful of the true meaning of Christmas. Forgive us when gifts become more important than the Giver. Gently remind us of the manger and the Christ child within, Your message of salvation, and truly the Lamb of God. These words were written in memory of Missy, a beloved young lady who meant the world to our family (December 5, 1993). Amen.

The Whisper of the Night

The darkness of the night yields as the sun's rays dance, intent on creating a masterpiece. Colors blend, spiraling upward and out, bathing the world in soft light as the promise of dawn unfolds. The rooster fills the pristine air with his jubilant voice, heralding the birth of another day as yet unscathed by the cares and demands that certainly will follow.

The young woman stirs, quietly slipping from the protective warmth of soft covers to kneel in prayer. Her faith, anchored in the very soul of her being, is as natural as drawing a breath.

The morning's first light illuminates the room as darkness slips away. Minute particles of dust dance on beams of light that seem but for a moment to visibly connect the creator to His world.

Her countenance of calm masks emotions that rise up and then slip away only to ascend to even greater heights. The mind reels with the message, balancing thoughts of imagination and reality yet knowing deep within she has encountered truth!

A tear silently escapes as the only outward sign that belies the wonder of words spoken, "Rejoice, highly favored one, the Lord is with you; blessed are you among women" (Luke 1:28). Falling on fabric of linen, it leaves but a trace to testify of its existence.

Questions, fears, thoughts of misunderstanding, and man's judgment tumble together in an array of wonder. However, the faith that found her worthy still hears the prophecy of the night, "And behold, you will conceive in your womb and bring forth a Son, and shall call His name Jesus. He will be great, and will be called the Son of the Highest, and the Lord God will give Him the throne of His father David" (Luke 1:31–32). That revelation holds her securely throughout her life.

Father, Mary was blessed with the whisper of prophecies given. Those at her side were blessed with prophecies fulfilled. Believers throughout the ages will be blessed to know these prophecies as truth. Amen.

CHAPTER 5

BEYOND THE ECLIPSE . . . WHERE INSPIRATION DAWNS

Finally, brethren, whatever things are true, whatever things are noble, whatever things are just, whatever things are pure, whatever things are lovely, whatever things are of good report, if there is any virtue and if there is anything praiseworthy—meditate on these things.
—Philippians 4:8

A Christening Prayer

The joy of new life touches each person within a place of worship, whether the ceremony is a christening, a baptism, or a dedication. One can almost hear the wings of angels moving ever-so-softly as the baby is cradled with loving arms. The precious drops of water interwoven with the holy words, "The Father, the Son, and the Holy Spirit," bring renewed peace to those who share this moment. The following prayer was written for a precious godchild.

Dear God, we would ask that You hear the prayer of this cherished child:

When tears fall, grace my parents with the ability to dry each one. When I stumble, provide my family with sure footing that comes from You. When questions arise, guide those who will walk at my side with answers that reflect Your wisdom. And Father, as I journey through this world created by Your hands, tuck these tiny fingers within Your capable grasp. Enable my words to voice praise worthy of You throughout the days and years to come. Amen.

A Voice Silenced

In my mind I still see silver hair that glistened like platinum. Faded memories remember a warm smile and tender words that held the ability to uplift those around her.

Serving on a church board was the perfect opportunity for a new friendship to flourish, but time constraints and more contemporary peers defined this writer's priorities. Looking back, conversations between us held little depth, disappearing almost as if they had never existed. My acquaintance remained just that, an acquaintance.

Why did I not take the time to inquire about the road of life upon which she traveled? What brought joy? It would have been a gift to know where her wisdom and humor, so beautifully possessed, had their beginnings? How much could have been gleaned from the challenges and adversities she overcame during her own youth. Her giving spirit would have willingly shared that early journey.

Now the wondering comes too late. Questions remain unasked. Moments cannot be recaptured once they have passed. Within our days, there are beginnings and endings. Minutes mark hours, and today moves toward tomorrow. I still wonder in the quiet of the night about what I missed because I took her presence for granted.

Why does one allow time to slip through fingers like grains of sand, realizing too late that a voice silenced is one no longer heard? If one could turn back time and make wiser decisions, perhaps life's regrets would not be as great. Did Christ not slow to hear His children? Their voices, their laughter, and their prayers have always been His concern. With Him as a role model, perhaps the influence of those whose lives wrap around our own would have the ability to forever change us.

Father, we thank You for the life of a friend who now rests. You always have time to explore the deepest recesses of the heart. Remind us to do the same. Enable us to realize what is sincerely important in each day... in each encounter. Amen.

Jim's Mountain

After a valiant climb through illness, you stood at the peak, looking forward to an unsurpassed view. You had visualized this healing within your heart for so long. Now within reach, the moment beckoned!

However, instead of eagles soaring and the gentle touch of the wind, you were confronted with grim reality. There was a new mountain looming in the distance, another battle to be fought. The prayer, "Father, where are You in all of this?" echoed across the expanse. In the quiet of the hour the answer was whispered, "In the midst with you, My child, in the midst."

While the world saw insurmountable mountains, there were those who stood near and marveled at your faith. You never ceased looking up. The beloved words of Isaiah 40:31, "But those who wait on the Lord Shall renew their strength; They shall mount up with wings like eagles, They shall run and not be weary, They shall walk and not faint," touched each of us with truth.

Your admirers now face their own journeys in days still before them. You can rest assured one by one, step by step, we will follow your lead. You were a wonderful role model, and we hold ever-so-tightly to the promise that the glorious view will be all we could ever imagine!

Father, my walk with a fellow believer through his own dark days inspired this story. Even when Your healing touch seemed elusive, Jim never doubted Your presence. Thank You for allowing me to be part of an inspirational journey that found its final destination at Your side. Amen.

Cherished Vows

How do I tell you that you're my heart? Words that have remained unspoken seem more comfortable in silence, as if I am unable to echo emotions deeply felt. I forever thank you for the gift of days filled with laughter and love. The vows we shared in a time now past have become promises fulfilled.

In the stillness one can hear, "For better or for worse." It is a gift to have received only the better. Your unselfish nature has been the foundation of a marriage richly blessed.

With the promise, "For richer or poorer," you have spoken truth. You believe that if one has happiness, he possesses immeasurable wealth!

"In sickness and in health" is grounded in a testimony that whatever the tragedies or sorrows encountered, we face them as one. When we found ourselves at the cross, encountering a loss so profound it forever changed us, we also glimpsed the treasured gift of our son's nineteen years. Together we found meaning in a life destined to be so brief.

Our years have not been without doubts, without questions. The one that always seems foremost in our minds is this: "If you ask anything in My name, I will do it" (John 14:14). The answer we saw as elusive is found in that still, small voice in the garden, "O My Father, if it is possible, let this cup pass from Me; nevertheless, not as I will, but as You will"(Matthew 26:39). Can we pray anything less as we walk with our creator?

If God were nonexistent, then the love I hold for you would be unfounded, for I learned it from Him. As each day brings renewed assurance of His presence, I will be at your side, cherishing a relationship freely given.

Heavenly Father, there is such depth in Jeremiah 29:11, "For I know the thoughts that I think toward you, says the Lord, thoughts of peace and not of evil, to give you a future and a hope." Those plans have truly been manifested in my life. Thank You for enabling me to face life's challenges with the gift of my beloved husband, truly a man after Your own heart. Amen.

The Road Traveled

Many never knew our son or reveled in his great sense of humor. I hope "The Road Traveled" will add insight as the steps of his journey are made known.

There are rare moments in time when God reveals His plan, unveiling things hidden. Slip back to the beginning of that moment in 1988. High school graduation from Blue Ridge School in Virginia had been celebrated, and college beckoned on the horizon.

One gift, a small mahogany frame, held beautiful calligraphy from Isaiah 40:31, "Those who wait on the Lord Shall renew their strength; They shall mount up with wings as eagles, They shall run and not grow weary, They shall walk and not faint." Adam was not familiar with the verse, but his manners dictated the response, "Thank you so much," just the same. He quipped that it was what he had always wanted along with his multitude of new Cross pens and personalized clipboards!

His journey commenced at the University of South Carolina. He loved college life, and it loved him. Whenever home, laughter and hometown friends were still part of this new life. One such trip reunited him with a young woman, and a friendship was forged. He spent time with her family, whose firm foundation was faith. The stained glass window that graced their family's home revealed their walk. "As for me and my house, we will serve the Lord" (Joshua 24:15, RSV). This was a new experience for us, but we found that solid life endearing where a family walked out their faith.

Life moved forward, and the friendship remained solid between our son and this family. Fast-forward to 1989 with one year of studies behind him. Adam started not feeling well, and in a matter of weeks, tests went from a possible virus to the discovery of a lung tumor.

As we waited for his physician late one evening, expecting the report to reveal an earlier opinion that there was no cause for concern, the phone in the room rang. It was his friend's dad, Mr. Barnhill, asking if he could come and pray with our son. If you knew our son's sense of humor, you might not have expected his response to be one of delight minus the banter that was sure to follow, yet the words, "That would be great," came without hesitation. Mike Barnhill drove ninety miles late in the evening and walked through Adam's hospital room door as the physician finished telling us the results were not good, that surgery would be scheduled immediately. We had unknowingly just become the recipients of God's perfect timing.

Mr. Barnhill knew God's nudges. He was so acquainted with his Lord through prayer that he obeyed this heart's command to drive through a dark night to be with a family that was reeling from news they never saw coming.

He asked Adam if he were a Christian and then led him to the Lord through Romans 10:9, "If you confess with your mouth the Lord Jesus and believe in your heart that God raised Him from the dead, you will be saved." The spirit does exult over each lost sheep that is found. The verse from Luke 15:6, 'Rejoice with me, for I have found my sheep which was lost!' was so evident throughout the dark night when joy overshadowed doubts and fears.

The tumor was removed, and recovery began. July 18, 1989, dawned, and health was reclaimed when the diagnosis given that day showed no signs of cancer. Life went quickly back to one of thankfulness, laughter, and college life.

Remember those words, "God reveals His plan?" A mere three months later symptoms resurfaced. There were subsequent tests and a diagnosis of brain tumors. This time Adam's walk became one of calm and trust as salvation was assured. God had known what lay ahead and was in each moment. We were reminded of that as a telegram arrived some months later from another friend, Claire,—the exact verse from

Isaiah 40:31! It confirmed that as we "waited upon the Lord," we were all held securely even through impenetrable darkness.

One year to the day of Adam reclaiming his health, on July 18, 1990, he slipped into God's presence.

The bronze plaque that stands vigil over his grave reads, "Isaiah 40:31: They shall mount up with wings as eagles." Through gifts of calligraphy, treasured friendships, telegrams, and a faith found, God truly did reveal His hand upon "The Road Traveled."

Lord, the plans we each encounter in life, whether making them... or enduring them, are orchestrated by You. When answers don't come as we hope or even accept, the whisper in Isaiah 55:9 continues to speak truth: "For as the heavens are higher than the earth, so are My ways higher than your ways and My thoughts than your thoughts." Surround us with the wisdom that is woven throughout that verse. Amen.

The Gift of Today

When time moves swiftly and the days held within months and years appear shorter than remembered, it gives one pause.

Where life once stretched toward forever, it now seems too brief, blurring the boundaries between spring and its promise of summer, fall and its shadow, winter. Emotions do swirl together like varied fragrances in a garden, as memories and hope seem to exist side by side.

Memories pull us back with the cadence "should have, would have, could have." The desire to recapture moments gone is a sentiment shared by many. It's not that we hesitate to embrace today, but there seems so much left undone in yesterday. Beloved, remember the past by embracing it and learning from it. Our merciful God reveals chances to right wrongs and to use words previously withheld to encourage. Forgiveness and encouragement allow us to learn from our past.

Remember, tomorrow will become the past in the blink of an eye! When the temptation comes to rush headlong into the future, reflect upon this jewel glistening in Psalm 118, "Praise God for the treasure that is uniquely today." The past is gone, and tomorrow has not yet come. We need to understand treasures bring joy *as* they are discovered moment by moment.

"This is the day the Lord has made; We will rejoice and be glad in it" (Psalm 118:24). Between the past that holds Calvary and the cross and the future with its beloved words, "I will come again," lays the precious gift we know as today. Embrace it!

God, words seem so inadequate in expressing our heartfelt gratitude for this new day. We ask for wisdom to use it wisely, strength to do Your will, and patience to savor the joy that awaits in laughter and friendship. Amen.

CHAPTER 6

BEYOND THE ECLIPSE . . . WHERE HOPE ABOUNDS

For I know the thoughts that I think toward you, says the Lord, thoughts of peace and not of evil, to give you a future and a hope.
—Jeremiah 29:11

A Gift Given

When laughter ceases, we will remember it is but for a season.

When memories dance across our minds recalling yesterday, we will hold dearly to the promise of tomorrow.

When tears flow unseen through hearts that yearn, we will cradle trust like a newborn lamb.

We will remember promises kept and prophecies fulfilled.

We will look up as stars grace the darkness.

We will know that the *true* gift of Christmas lay within that manger.

Lord, the star beckoned shepherds and wise men to the One revealed in prophecy. May those who still seek find this treasured gift within their own lives. Amen and amen.

Glimpses of Hope

What is this thing called hope?

It is the rainbow after the rains have ended.

It is the laughter after the tears have dried.

It has caused shepherds to seek and wise men to journey.

It comforted Mary as she held her beloved Son and enabled Peter to move past the denials.

What is this thing called hope?

It is when one stands at the tomb now empty.

It is when one looks at the cross and sees far, far beyond.

God, hope seems so attainable when things are good, less certain when the darkness comes. Remind us always that You are in each day and each life. Amen.

A Stone, a Tomb, and Hope

The days are now past with waving palm branches gone and crowds silenced. The crosses have been taken away, and those who shattered the night with their taunts are no more.

The stillness stands as an unseen sentry while the tears of those who mourn journey from the heart. Surely this is the soul's darkest hour! Dreams have died, and hope seems lost. Yet even in the darkness, the words of the psalmist ring of prophesy, words that were woven together long before the cross. "Why are you cast down, O my soul? And why are you disquieted within me? Hope in God; For I shall yet praise Him, The help of my countenance and my God" (Psalm 42:11).

We would do well to remember those words as we reflect upon Easter morning. We rejoice that the stone no longer stands guard and the tomb echoes with emptiness. We hear truth in the whisper of the psalmist, "Hope in God," a hope that for all eternity will not disappoint.

Father, praises abound for bringing us past the cross and allowing us to see the other side. The hope in Psalms is ours today because of Calvary. Amen.

Lessons in Perfection

Lessons taught, lessons learned! Each day brings opportunities to see God's hand upon our lives as the Holy Spirit reveals remembrances of things long-forgotten.

I recall, as if it were yesterday, being with my mother in a restaurant when a migrant worker and his small child came through the door. They sat at a table and ordered a glass of cold water, resting from the heat of the day. My mother paused long enough to grasp the situation. She recognized the father's money could not be spared for a meal out, that hunger would have to wait. The little one with his dusty overalls and a tattered shirt obediently drank his water, never asking for the bounty he saw around him. With a solemn whisper to the manager, my mother enabled needs to be met. I know that very afternoon the father and his small son experienced not a handout but compassion and the fact that people do care. I learned from the best as God's voice resounded with quiet dignity, "Assuredly, I say to you, inasmuch as you did it to one of the least of these My brethren, you did it to Me" (Matthew 25:40).

The Holy Spirit continued His lesson by revealing the memory of being with my dad on a cold Ohio night on December 6. It was my birthday, and the custom of choosing my very own gift was tradition. You can picture a child's enthusiasm and excitement. I have since forgotten the gift, but I clearly remember that night. The present had been found, and the rest of the evening lay ahead with special time for the two of us. Then out of the blue my dad encountered a man on the street. We didn't have the term *homeless*, but that would have been an apt description. My dad proceeded to invite that gentleman along with this wide-eyed child into a bar where we ordered meals and ate. I wondered why he didn't just give the man some money. After all, in a little girl's eyes, it was a special time with my dad, not my mother, my brothers, and certainly not a stranger, a questionable one at that!

But you see, my father knew cash would not be spent on a nourishing hot meal, so we sat together over dinner, my dad chatting away as if this were an everyday occurrence. I can still hear God's whisper, "Inasmuch as you did it to one of the least of these My brethren, you did it to Me."

From parents whose faith went beyond words in a book and church on Sunday mornings, I witnessed a goal worthy of Matthew 5:48, "Therefore you shall be perfect, just as your Father in heaven is perfect."

My parents were not blessed with long lives. My dad died of a heart attack at fifty-six, and my mother passed away from cancer after her sixtieth birthday. Although they weren't given an abundance of years, their lives forever impacted their children and generations still future. They left the world a gentler place through their caring. One such legacy was a daughter who watched, listened, and through their examples, grew in faith, becoming a bit more learned in the ways one should respond to a hurting world.

God's message is so simple even a child can understand. We are commanded to reach out, comfort, love, and make a difference. Whether it is in a restaurant or on a bustling street, opportunities are always within reach of the heart.

Remember, we do have the quintessential role model. Jesus walked where we walk. He experienced this world. He knew rejection, pain, and want firsthand. God never asks anything of us that He did not first ask of His Son. Jesus was perfect, as we are called to be perfect. When we stumble, when circumstances allow fear or apathy to overshadow what is right, we can seek forgiveness and begin anew each and every time. We are for now less than perfect... but remember, we have not yet completed the race. When our life here is finished, we will be like Him, perfect... at last!

Father, Your faithfulness is never-ending as things now past impact the way we see those around us. Through the example of Jesus, we strive toward a clean and perfect heart. We boldly ask that our actions toward others will reflect that still, small voice, "Inasmuch as you did it to the least of these My brethren, you did it to Me." Amen.

Sun and Surf

This devotional tagged along during a trip to the coast for a youth group.

Early morning dawns on surfers drifting upon boards of fiberglass, paddling toward the promise of a long ride. It finds fishermen standing in the surf, casting out, patiently waiting for the strike that is sure to come.

As they watch the sun rise in the sky, do they reflect upon the One who created it all? Do they realize He is always there? Do the words "Good morning" greet Him? It is so easy to run ahead and forget He enjoys your company. He would love to come along as you surf, fish, or just walk upon His carpet of sand. Include Him in your conversations and allow Him to share in your laughter.

He loves being at your side, basking in a time set apart for you and your friends. These early years sometimes come with the expectations that they will always be. However, days will slip past, and friendships will change as time moves toward your future. Remember, there will be one true companion throughout your lives, one always within reach.

Say, "Good morning, Father," and let the day begin!

Lord, we are thankful for the gift of today. It holds fond recollections of our beach family and their love of surfboards, sand, and boats. We know yesterday is past and tomorrow is not yet here. Forgive us when we forget to invite You upon our journey. Please know there is always room in our hearts and our lives for You. Amen.

The Suitcase

Throughout the centuries the words of Jesus, "Come, take up the cross, and follow Me," have enticed those who would listen. This command from Mark 10:21 offers direction when life's paths seem to wind aimlessly with no clear destination in sight.

The Holy Spirit imparts a yearning within the listener to know God, to walk at His side. When the listener is also the one seeking, there is an even greater desire to walk this beckoning road. God's understanding of the doubt that lived within the heart of Thomas and His mercy when Peter's denials rang out are but a few of the intricate gems revealed along the way. Those disciples stand among countless followers who harken this message.

With the words "follow Me," the seeker embarks upon a journey that promises to be life-changing. Imagine his confusion when he notices the suitcase by his side. Perhaps God misunderstands. (New seekers do sometimes assume God is not all-knowing.) He certainly will not need luggage to make this trek. Within his spirit, God speaks, "You never seem to be without this burden. You carry it wherever you go. I know it will be a hindrance, but it seems to be such a part of you."

The suitcase is quickly becoming something beyond an encumbrance. What could it possibly represent? Does the seeker dare open it, or could the contents prove too overwhelming to bear? He is tempted to drag it along, as that has to be easier than dealing with what's inside. You see, once opened, the light will reveal its contents.

The seeker knows that to respond to the words "follow Me," he must trust God. If he acknowledges the verse in Philippians 4:13, "I can do all things through Christ who strengthens me," or the wisdom of Genesis 18:14, "Is anything too hard for the Lord?" then the suitcase must be considered.

With much trepidation, it is unlatched. Its contents overflow, as they are finally released from the constraints of that musty old suitcase. On the top are needs yet to be met and comforts yet to be given. Good intentions weigh a lot and tend to accumulate if follow-through does not occur. They become part of the baggage that is carried, heavy and worthless.

Beneath those unused intentions are empty flower vases. The vision of an orderly suitcase is quickly vanishing! Why are these items even there? God reminds the seeker that so many times he does not visit friends in need because he does not want to go with empty hands. God shares a precious secret. Those waiting only want his smile, his touch. The scripture "I was sick and you visited me" (Matthew 25:36) echoes among the fragments.

The suitcase is starting to feel lighter as its contents are unearthed. There are weights of bitterness, frustration, anger, anxiety, and yes, even unbelief. God is never shocked, as our thoughts are forever shared with Him. At times the pain and disappointments are too much to bear, and the seeker secures the latch for another day. God understands, as it is not a day's journey but one that takes a lifetime. Step by step, things are unpacked and removed that hide joy and hinder laughter.

You might assume that the suitcase is no longer on this journey, that the seeker now follows his Lord unencumbered. In life, however, the reality of baggage is never far. Some days its lightness makes one forget it is there, holding only good memories and contentment; on other days the sheer weight of things like regret and remorse fill it to the brim.

By heeding the words "follow Me," the cherished seeker finally understands the burden of that suitcase is no longer carried alone but entrusted to the One most capable of leading.

Father, when weariness overwhelms and thoughts seem to tumble with no clear direction, You're the compass. We ask with the boldness of those seeking that the Holy Spirit reveal the contents of our own infamous suitcases, releasing burdens that weigh down this journey called life. In Christ's name, amen.

CHAPTER 7

BEYOND THE ECLIPSE . . . WHERE STRENGTH IS REFLECTED

But those who wait on the Lord Shall renew their strength;
They shall mount up with wings like eagles, They shall
run and not be weary, They shall walk and not faint.
—Isaiah 40:31

A Walk in the Valley

The hands of time move so slowly as if to cease their journey. The words of the prayer formed in the mind remain held in the heart, silent and still. Formidable mountains that loom in the distance are shadowed with a hope that they truly do not exist.

One who has faced devastating words knows they possess the ability to forever change life. In God's mercy those words begin to carry less weight as one year merges into another while we encounter the medical jargon NED, meaning "no evidence of disease". Then like a shiver that travels down one's spine, another illness seems to surface. Tests and more challenges take center stage as the wait begins anew.

Sometimes children of faith find themselves in darkness where light seems elusive and the mountain insurmountable. In that darkness, the fear that threatens to overwhelm thrusts one into a place like no other. When one sees no path, trust becomes everything upon this mountaintop.

However, time does travel onward, and on *this* journey the mountain is brought low when the threat vanishes. We find ourselves no longer balancing on the peak. We have returned to the valley, where footing is sure. The One who stood silently in the darkness still walks at our sides.

Now we understand. No matter what this life holds, the warmth of His hand is everything.

Father, a trial faced by a dear friend became a distant memory that was left in the past, no longer impacting the future. We are thankful for the gift of mercy, enabling Your child to find firm footing in the valley. Amen.

By Word of Mouth

Words are the gift of speech from our creator. Those early words in Genesis 1:3, "Let there be light," speak the universe into existence. Their power ushers in a world where God's majesty is portrayed by stars at twilight and planets that journey far yet never stray.

The creation of man in His image is to be His finest masterpiece, enabling cherished conversations to connect the creator to His world. Words begin to flow. Language, much like a river, encounters plateaus on its journey. These plateaus are places of calm where laughter rings true and crystal clear pools mirror a serenity that one can reach out and almost touch. One would prefer to remain where this peace reigns. Such a place is a garden called Eden, where love flourishes as God walks with His children.

Sadly, reality overtakes this peace. Mountains rising in the distance symbolize man's fall into sin. Water becomes tumultuous as thrusts of power drive it through crevasses and down canyons, altering all it encounters. Threatening words echo turmoil as hate takes root in the heart of man.

Words now have another facet, as revealed in Genesis 4:9, "Then the Lord said to Cain, 'Where is Abel your brother?' He said, 'I do not know. Am I my brother's keeper?'" Cain's words of malice reveal a heart hardened by jealously and murder.

Words of destruction begin to flow through time, leaving devastation in their wake. The brutal death of John the Baptist and the stoning of Stephen become reality! A voice created to talk with the Father and pray for our brother now has a darker side. Our sense of hearing seems to be assaulted by the cadence of so many words running together. You can visualize life careening out of control as words meant for glory become words of wrath.

Listen as the tranquil sounds of the river mingle with human voices. John baptizes Jesus and God's voice transcends centuries with the proclamation, "This is *My* beloved Son, in whom I am well pleased" (Matthew 3:17). Yet in darker moments, we hear the vicious cries, "Blasphemer."

The joyous cries of hosanna and the rustling of palm branches accompany Christ as He makes His triumphant entry into Jerusalem. This joy becomes overshadowed by words of unfathomable hatred when the chief priests and officers cried out, "Crucify Him, crucify Him" (John 19:6).

Peter's allegiance for his friend is declared at the Mount of Olives, "Even if all are made to stumble because of You, I will never be made to stumble"(Matthew 26:33). Almost in the same breath, fear intrudes and his words pierce the night, "I do not know the Man" (Matthew 26:74).

Jesus' beloved prayer, "Father, forgive them, for they know not what they do" (Luke 23:34), collides with the cruel taunt, "He saved others; Himself He cannot save. If He is the King of Israel, let Him now come down from the Cross, and we will believe Him" (Matthew 27:42).

The crescendo of the crucifixion encounters a silence so deafening the soul recoils. No words will ever be written to fully allow man to comprehend what transpired on Calvary.

Take heart. That same voice that echoes darkness also embraces words of light. Mark 16:6 says, "Do not be alarmed. You seek Jesus of Nazareth, who was crucified. He is risen. He is not here. See the place where they laid Him." With those words, "He is risen," truth is heralded! We must now ask ourselves if the words from our lips bring life... or death.

All we do, all we are, all we hope to become as God's children is still at the mercy of the spoken word. Beloved, only God can tame the tongue. We would do well to remember the command in Mark 4:39, "Then He arose and rebuked the wind, and said to the sea, 'Peace, be still'. And the wind ceased and there was great calm." As Jesus calmed the raging storm on the Galilean Sea, we must trust Him to restrain those rivers within us that threaten to overflow. Pray that His grace quenches anger, frustration, and hate. Allow His mercy to replenish spirits with gentleness, compassion, and love.

Father, enable us to hear truth so that we might come to terms with the rivers of speech that course through us. Grant us insight to know words do have the power to bless or curse. With our voices, we ask the Holy Spirit to lead us. May we forever choose love when hate abounds, extend forgiveness when condemnation beckons, and lift up praise worthy of You. Amen.

Creation: A Reflection
of the Heart

What has man done with God's precious gift of creation? Time is showing us a world spinning toward extinction with oceans tainted, neglected. We see a sky created to gently surround and caress that grows ominously dark. Cherished animals so dearly named by God's creation of man, Adam, no longer exist.

Perhaps this image of our world reflects the heart of man, a heart laden with man's definition of morality. Do we find ourselves slipping farther away from God and the desires He holds for His children? Is it possible that our love for one another has been overshadowed by the defiant words of Cain when the Lord asked, "Where is Abel your brother?" and he said, "I do not know. Am I my brother's keeper?" (Genesis 4:9).

Do we no longer feel the yearning of a soul that seeks? Perhaps hope and compassion truly can slip away so quietly that, like God's gift of this world, one will not realize it until they are gone.

Father, only by the love of the precious Holy Spirit are we able to see beyond ourselves. Enable us to care not only for this world but also for Your children whose paths cross our own. Draw us to those who yearn, gently reminding us we are not yet home. Amen.

Flight

The shadow of the eagle touches the land as he glides upon the breath of the wind. As wisps of air lift him like glimmers of hope, one can almost hear the quiet words from Isaiah 40:31, "But those who wait on the Lord Shall renew their strength; They shall mount up with wings like eagles, They shall run and not be weary, They shall walk and not faint." Oh, to always glide upward, soaring to new heights as the spirit touches the soul!

The operative word within this scripture is *wait*. How difficult that seems when nights are long and days endless. How challenging to be still when answers tarry; to heed those whispers of steadfastness from the Holy Spirit.

The solitary sentry is *faith*. He stands firm as fears abound and tears seem to flow unbidden. He is able to withstand the barrage of words—what if, if only, and why. He alone embraces the patience to await the precious wind that enables one to 'mount up with wings like eagles,' soaring above sadness and despair.

Standing alongside, the Creator's enfolding arms give a comfort that restores the heart, enabling one to complete a journey orchestrated since the beginning of time.

God, time will take us to destinations as yet unknown. We ask for the depth of wisdom to see beyond today. We pray for an ever deepening faith that reminds us time spent with You is but a glimpse of eternity. Amen.

The Letter

Sometimes in the still of the night, one discovers a letter written in the heart. This letter is to those who put aside their own lives to care for others who need God's word:

> Dearest children,
>
> I want to encourage you with words from Matthew 25:21, His lord said to him, 'Well done, good and faithful servant; you were faithful over a few things, I will make you ruler over many things. Enter into the joy of your lord.'
>
> I know you can be trusted with the message of the gospel to a world that seems lost and dark. As others plant their flowers and pursue their elusive dreams, you remain steadfast in the eternal things with which you have been entrusted.
>
> As I could have chosen by My Father's free will to have remained in the security of My carpentry profession and at the side of My beloved mother, you also could choose to remain in the safe haven of your private, personal lives. As I knew those whom I had not yet met needed to hear of My Father's love, you also have considered it a privilege to respond to the gentle command, "Feed My sheep" (John 21:17).
>
> Thank you for caring, sharing, and embarking upon a walk that truly is life-changing!

The signature on this letter simply reads:

With love,
The Shepherd

Lord, Your whisper was heard! This message encourages those that any labor done in Your name has value. The praise one receives from men pales in comparison with those words, "Well done, good and faithful servant," giving hearts joy beyond measure. Selah.

The Tears of the Eagle

With the muffled refrain, "America, America," the broad stripes and bright stars fade into the distance. The symbolic eagle that soars above is no longer within sight, his majesty hidden. In the breath of a moment, the unimaginable has become reality as planes plummet and towers crumble. Can the words "God shed His grace on thee" still be heard among the sorrow and darkness? Are His children worthy? Are those He has called to Himself even faithful?

As beliefs throughout the ages continue to clash, Christians are the ones who stand at a tomb now empty. When hatred and intolerance insist on their own way, we cling to the words of Jesus, "I am the way, the truth, and the life. No one comes to the Father except through Me" (John 14:6). For us, that *is* truth. That *is* enough.

As Christians embrace revelation with the words of Philippians 2:10–11, "That at the name of Jesus every knee should bow, of those in heaven, and of those on earth, and of those under the earth, and that every tongue should confess that Jesus Christ is Lord, to the glory of God the Father," the eagle shall soar to even greater heights. His tears, gently tended by God gracious hand, will no longer fall. May we ever embrace the words from the Pledge of Allegiance, "One nation under God!"

Lord, we will forever remember September 11, 2001, and the way it impacted our beloved country, shaped our perceptions, and reminded us of a voice that can never be stilled—Yours! Amen.

CHAPTER 8

BEYOND THE ECLIPSE . . . WHERE SALVATION REIGNS

For God so loved the world that He gave His only begotten Son, that whoever believes in Him should not perish but have everlasting life.
—John 3:16

A Beloved Prayer

The prayer is whispered as the night stands still, "The hour has come that the Son of Man should be glorified" (John 12:23). The breeze seems to cease, as if straining to hear those words. The full moon of Passover casts its silvery light upon the men gathered.

One can see the figures of those who have drawn close over the past three years. Peter, John, Matthew, James, and the others are there, but the attention is on the one praying. His words reflect knowledge of a journey that is drawing to a close. "The hour has come."

The words of Jesus reveal His intimacy with the Father. They portray the love He has for those who have walked at His side—men who were gifts of friendship when the world would meet its Messiah. They watched in awe as the blind saw and the lame walked. They witnessed Lazarus being raised from the dead. Now they listen intently to their master's prayer.

However, in His mind, He can already hear the soldiers marching, the lashes of the whip, and the denials of His beloved Peter. He can feel nails driven and the crown of thorns that will adorn His head as king. He knows that on Golgotha stands the cross. His heart can sense the grief of Mary and the scattering of His beloved sheep.

One might think these images would overwhelm His thoughts, leaving only room for fear and despair, yet the words of the prayer continue to flow uninterrupted. One can hear the unconditional love, "I pray for them. I do not pray for the world but for those whom You have given Me, for they are Yours" (John 17:9).

Even as destiny resounds with jeers, taunts, and the words Jesus alone can hear, "Away with Him, away with Him! Crucify Him" (John

19:15), His countenance reveals the heart. He is well aware as darkness turns day into night, the voice crying, "It is finished" (John 19:30), will be His own. His prayer continues, cascading like a waterfall over the generations of believers still to come, "I do not pray for these alone, but also for those who will believe in Me through their word" (John 17:20).

Beloved, remember those precious words and the One who prayed them. He asked His heavenly Father to hold and sustain us when the world would dare take all we possess.

You see, Jesus knew that after the hopelessness of the dark night, there would be a dawn, where splendid golden rays would illuminate a new day. The beloved prayer that had its beginning before the cross, "Father, the hour has come that the Son of Man should be glorified" (John 12:23), would have an answer as the joyous shout, "He is risen," echoes throughout eternity (Mark 16:6).

Father, the Good Shepherd truly looked after His sheep. Amen.

A Friend for Life

March draws to a close as winter fades into the past. Tender green leaves begin their ascent toward the heavens as time slows for a moment. Friends who are as varied as the colors of the promised spring slip into our thoughts. Reflect upon those who have walked at your side. Some left small traces of memories, now faded and distant; others touched your very soul, forever impacting who you are and what you've become.

As one ponders friends and friendships, those who walked with Jesus become the pulse of our story. Journey down the road to Jerusalem and stand at the foot of a staircase. Listen with your heart.

Voices mingle, and snatches of conversations can be heard as sandals glide across the floor of clay. The door opens and closes as friends gather. The men converse in small groups, whispering, as if to speak aloud will bring the future upon them before they can bear it. Do they know how significant this gathering will be? *This Last Supper—*

The acts recorded for all eternity will symbolize wine as blood and bread the body broken. Much will be revealed in one room, one evening.

Come, climb the stairs leading to the upper room. Listen to the men who have walked with one another. Has it been just three years? One can hardly grasp a time when they were not together. Friendships that were forged now seem to have always existed. Time beckons as we become onlookers of truth.

John's brow, knit with emotion, mirrors the thoughts that carry him back to their first encounter, replaying the words that went unspoken. Who was this slight man, not really handsome in appearance? On this day of days, perhaps John alone senses the heaviness that weighs upon the heart of Jesus. Oh, to be able to reach out, to reassure John that as supper ends and he steps into a future that does not include his dearest friend, there is so much more, that there will be a tomorrow!

See the large burly man near the table? It can only be Peter! He is all one would imagine. His thoughts swirl and spin as he grapples with this talk of betrayal. Why, he would die for his friend! So lost in thought, he almost misses the word *denial*. We want to share with Peter that even when darkness comes, the dawn will be majestic beyond imagination. We want to reassure him that the word *forgiveness* will bring joy as despair flees.

Silently we remain and are drawn by another who seems to stand apart. He is called Judas. His thoughts are a tumbling mass of contradictions. He has seen the sick healed, sight restored, and the dead brought back to life. However, betrayal has taken root in this heart that saw truth and looked away. The price of that betrayal? Thirty pieces of silver! The sound of each coin echoes so loudly in his mind that he fears all can hear. Did Jesus just speak? We are in the far reaches of the room, yet we hear His words clearly, "Most assuredly, I say to you, one of you will betray Me"(John 13:21). Oh, Judas, turn back. The end will destroy your soul. Choosing friendship that the world offers, he rises quickly to meet his destiny. Tears quietly fall from those of us who can only stand and watch.

Mesmerized, we feel a part of this room and the drama unfolding. Almost imperceptibly we choose sides, choose friends. We are drawn toward John and Peter and away from Judas. We assure ourselves that we would stand with Jesus, that we would become the friend who stayed.

Remember, beloved, we possess human qualities and limitations much like the disciples. We are reminded of these weaknesses as the twelve become eleven and we glimpse Golgotha on the horizon.

If you want a friend for life, choose wisely. Rather than waiting for our search to find Him, this creator of the universe reached down and claimed us. His friendship has gone the distance… to Calvary and back. His presence reflects light when darkness comes. He is the One who is always there, so close that He dwells in the heart of every believer.

God, when the world entices us with its promises of friendship, help us to see beyond the pieces of silver. Remind us that we love because You first loved us, that You live in the hearts of those who choose to call You friend. Amen.

The Encounter

Those long ago encountered a man who wore sandals as He traveled dusty roads and donned a robe that gave warmth on a journey that spanned thirty-three years. One wonders if they assumed He was just a craftsman who worked with His hands. He truly did turn discarded lives into beauty! His majesty enabled Him to see that "diamond in the rough" others would have summarily dismissed as worthless.

One ponders if this rare meeting would have been well received or viewed as unimportant. This very real encounter did take fishermen to Calvary. It led Judas to infamy and resulted in the Isle of Patmos for John. Its value is beyond measure. It guided an adulteress into forgiveness when condemnation reigned and transformed the lives of those who stood at an empty tomb.

For some who paused but for a moment, it may have been perceived as a chance encounter. For those who realized they were in the presence of someone unlike any other, it became life-changing. When we become still enough to hear the soft, sandaled footsteps and the rustling of His robe, we are blessed with an encounter that will lead into eternity.

God, thank You for Jesus. It never fails to astound us that He has made all the difference in an unrelenting world. How blessed we have been to not only know and love Him but to be forever changed by His touch. Make us mindful that He brings depth into our lives. Let us never take this cherished presence for granted in a world that oftentimes overlooks things of value. Amen.

The Lamb

The precious lamb, newly born, wobbles on legs that seem somehow out of proportion with this body of woolen clothing. As he marvels at a world so fresh and new, sights and sounds swirl around him in a delicious sense of wonder. So this is the world spoken into existence so long ago! The words "Let there be light" (Genesis 1:3) take on a whole new dimension.

As sunlight streams through the trees, playing off leaves and branches, the rays dance, creating a symphony of beauty. The cascading waterfall shimmers like diamonds as birds raise their voices in song. Butterflies glide among the flowers, allowing the lamb to glimpse the delicate beauty of their wings with patterns of intricate color.

A world waits to be explored with so much to be accomplished in the time appointed. A sense of urgency tugs at his heart as he perceives the task for which he was sent, yet it is brushed aside for the moment. The lamb is young and the time of fulfillment is still future.

The excitement of this day gives way to weariness as the little lamb seeks a safe haven under a tree, a sapling actually. The twig like branch that pierces the soil has but a leaf or two, revealing newness in vivid color. With barely a nod, the infant lamb finds a bed under the bough of that sapling. Curling up, tucking spindly legs beneath him, he leans against his newfound friend for comfort as a relationship takes root.

These days are rich with encounters. The lamb explores the world close at hand, sharing that which lies beyond the sapling's limited boundaries. In return, giving comfort and shelter, the tree patiently waits, knowing as night falls, his friend will return to his side. The bond deepens as whispers fill the nights before sleep overtakes.

As years pass, the lamb begins to journey the road set before him, fulfilling prophecies of long ago. His now able legs carry him to appointments with destiny. There's the baptism with John at the river's edge, a wedding feast where wine is the miracle of the day, an encounter with the woman at the well, even a conflict of wills as money changers exit the temple, followed by tumbling cages and clattering coins!

The sapling, now a stately proud tree, waits as a sentry, rejoicing when the lamb returns from his pilgrimages. Memories are shared, and laughter rings clear as they recall the infant lamb clinging to the precariously new sapling for comfort and security, delighting in a friendship that has blossomed over the years.

They yearn for time to stand motionless in the sweetness of these days. However, the future beckons and time must travel onward. As prophecies approach fulfillment, taking the lamb farther from home, the tree experiences a loneliness that is all but unbearable. His branches bend in sorrow as nights blend one into another, yet he never ceases to search longingly for a glimpse of his friend.

He perceives his companion has a calling—a ministry perhaps—to take the message of hope, healing, and forgiveness to a world beyond the meadow. You see, he knows his stationary nature dictates that he cannot follow. He must content himself with messages the breeze carries, hearing stories resounding throughout the land. By the touch of the lamb, lepers are being made whole, the blind receive their sight, and the deaf hear. There's even the report of a man called Lazarus being raised from the dead! Can this be? Could the little lamb possess such wondrous gifts? Why only God Himself could bestow these!

A reunion that is destined to be their last finds the lamb weary and burdened under the protective branches of one who has always stood by his side. Sometimes when stillness seems to lengthen the night, the tree senses weavings of conversations of which he is not a part. The precious lamb appears to draw close to someone visible only to himself. Is it imagination… or does someone hear? On that eve the boughs seem to draw closer, creating a canopy that, if possible, would hide his friend.

Peace cannot last. The solitude is shattered! The world has come for the gentle lamb.

If a tree could cry, the sound would pierce the very soul. His beloved friend's quiet resolve speaks volumes as his eyes glance back over their time together. Thirty-three years now seem but a moment.

While others flee and denials echo through the night, the lamb is taken. Prophecy hurtles toward its hour with destiny.

There is but one final role in which the majestic tree will be forced to play a part. It is his fate to become the cross. As he is felled by men and destroyed by an act of hate, he glimpses Calvary on the horizon. Boughs that so lovingly sheltered the lamb now are forced to lift him up.

The whisper "It is finished" (John 19:30) ushers in the darkness. Yet as Easter morning dawns, it brings a glory unequaled as words resound from the empty tomb, "He is risen. He is risen" (Mark 16:6). It is a proclamation of victory that for all eternity will change how man perceives death.

Take heart, beloved. If you journey but a short distance, where flowers bloom and butterflies dance, you will encounter a stump. Look closely and be blessed. Life is renewed as a tiny shoot makes its way toward heaven.

Father, I truly felt each word was a prayer as I penned "The Lamb." I am forever grateful for the powerful words placed within my heart. Amen and amen.

Viewpoints

The world would see Him as a carpenter, yet He did not build the cross. He built friendships and a legacy of truth that would throughout time exist.

The world would see Him as a shepherd, yet He stood not at watch in distant fields. His sheep were those who gave hearts willingly to the One who would never stop searching for His own.

The world would see Him as king of the Jews, yet He never graced an earthly throne. His kingdom had for a time been left behind so His children could walk at His side and be blessed by His touch.

Yes, the world that stood on Golgotha would see Him as powerless and defeated. What they did not understand was that it was for them and that Easter would come.

Father, the scripture verse "I am the good shepherd. The good shepherd gives His life for the sheep" (John 10:11) is especially vivid during the Easter season. Let our lives reflect how we see You and our actions mirror Your love... because of Calvary. Amen.

The Invitation

With Easter on the horizon, memories of the Last Supper caress our thoughts. We see bread broken and wine shared as we confront betrayal and intimacy almost in a single breath. Words of prophecy and hope seem interwoven on that evening so long ago.

Beloved, even though the Last Supper is past and those who surrounded the table gone, the truth remains. The Shepherd's table still exists!

Revelation assures us with its timeless message that the table continues to beckon as the guest list is written and invitations sent. These poignant words from Revelation 3:20, "Behold, I stand at the door and knock," portray an image like no other. Sunday school lessons bring recollections of Jesus standing in a white robe with His hand softly knocking. We sometimes miss the symbolism surrounding that ancient door. The side portrayed in a painting has no handle. Only the one standing *within* has the ability to open it. The scripture continues with the words, "If anyone hears My voice and *opens* the door, I will come in to him and dine with him, and he with Me."

In a life filled with so much, does one take time to accept the invitation to dine with the Master, or does the fleeting brilliance of *this* world keep Him just outside the door? Do we not realize but for a few precious feet, He would be at our side?

Father, we know the table waits! We boldly ask Your Holy Spirit to awaken within us the desire to ask You into our hearts. By our willingness to open that door, the acceptance of this invitation will be life-changing. Amen.

BELOVED PHOTOGRAPHS

Before the eclipse, long before the shadow slipped across that circle of light, these images were captured. There seemed all the time in the world to embrace the days and laughter held within the lens of that camera.

When an eclipse takes that sunshine and memories seem destined to live behind sorrow, photographs hold their own unique ability to scatter the darkness! With rays of joy, they bear witness to all those cherished yesterdays that held Adam's smile and his presence.

Glimpses of laughter can be found among the grains of sand with Adam and Adrian and their cousins, Kristin, Jason, and Megan in Key Biscayne, Florida

Good buddies on Topsail Island, NC, in the 1970s!

(Left to right: Kristin Harrold Leggett, Megan Harrold Latham,
Adam, Jason Harrold, and Adrian Harrold Wood)

Adrian penned this treasured message under the much-loved photo of her big brother, Adam, with his tomatoes!

ADRIAN AND THOMAS WOOD

I have always loved this picture . . . an image of a sunny, tan, happy little boy proud of his daddy's red tomatoes!

It is a reminder to me of a brother that made my life so wonderful and my growing up an experience that was truly God's work. As a mother, I feel better-equipped to make the lives of my children wonderful and full of love and God's presence. May we always know that pleasures need only come from a bucket of ripe tomatoes.

All my love,
Adrian

The story "Adam Always Liked You Best" originated with these early pictures of Adam with his beloved sister, Adrian.

A favorite photograph of Adam and Adrian . . .

Adam's 19th birthday celebrated with Adrian at his side!

Joy existed behind a foreign column on a journey to faraway lands, capturing the poignant smile that defined our son!

A busy square in Salzburg, Austria, was a perfect venue for those Ray-Ban sunglasses!

A picture has the ability to hold within its grasp three beloved generations for all time! 1988 Blue Ridge School (Virginia) graduation with Adam, his dad, Blair Harrold, and his papa, Ray Harrold

Latham Jenkins, Adam's friend from Blue Ridge School, took this photograph by their campus pond one brisk winter day. For all the years we have known Latham, he has never been far from his camera! He now lives in Jackson Hole, WY, and continues to be a wonderful part of our family along with his wife, Megan, and children, Jack and Genevieve. We are grateful for this treasured portrayal of Adam as seen through Latham's eyes. © Latham Jenkins/ Circ.biz

Enjoying a first-class view of the cockpit with his cousin, Jason Harrold (in the borrowed hat), while on the ultimate spring break from the University of South Carolina! Still wondering to this day how they gained access . . .

Katie Wright's unwavering love and encouragement for each of us was chronicled in the story "Treasures of the Heart."

Adam's namesake, Adam Russell Harrold Wood, doing what he does best, interacting with one of God's creatures at Seaquarium in Key Biscayne, Florida.

These children whom Uncle Adam never got to meet still reflect his vibrant personality and impish smile. As new memories are created, he would love being included in the many conversations and Adam stories. What blessings they are as they grow up in a family of which he was so proud!

The ultimate Thanksgiving photograph where blessings truly can be counted! The printing presses were held until November 9, 2013, so young Amos could take his place among these pages with his parents and those gregarious siblings.

EPILOGUE

For those who pause to see what is tucked behind a camera's lens or within the pages of a book, images can be transformed into friends one would have embraced had the opportunities been given. God places others upon our journey to impact and encourage us. I pray that He will enfold you within His capable arms, not only through the eclipses encountered in this life, but far, far beyond . . .

ABOUT THE AUTHOR

The journey from Ohio State University to North Carolina and beyond brought ALICE THORPE HARROLD and husband Blair through deep sorrow and great joy. Their daughter, Adrian, son-in-law, Thomas, and grandchildren Thomas, Adam Russell, Anne Blair, and William Amos Benbury Wood bring sunlight into each day!

Made in the USA
Monee, IL
17 September 2023

42902142R10080